TOPSY-TURVY TRACY

The Upside-Dowɴᴇʀ Day

written by Susie Taylor

illustrated by Tammie Lyon

Zonder**kidz**

Zonderkidz®

The children's group of Zondervan

www.zonderkidz.com

Topsy-Turvy Tracy: The Upside-Downer Day
Copyright © 2004 by Susie Taylor
Illustrations copyright © 2004 by Tammie Lyon

Requests for information should be addressed to:
Zonderkidz, Grand Rapids, Michigan 49530

ISBN: 0-310-70442-1

The Library of Congress cataloged this book under the Library of Congress
Control Number 2003018612.

Editor: Gwen Ellis
Art direction and interior design: Michelle Lenger

Printed in China
04 05 06 07/HK/4 3 2 1

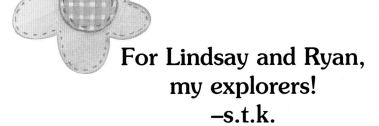

For Lindsay and Ryan,
my explorers!
–s.t.k.

For Robin, who helps keep my days right side up.
Thanks for being such a great friend!
–t.l.

Tracy was a little girl
No bigger than a minute,
And each day she explored God's world
And all the things within it!

Today was no exception,
An adventure was at hand.
In God's world lots can happen.
It's a part of his great plan.

But instead of getting out of bed
And landing on her feet,
Tracy got out upside down,
Her foot caught in the sheet.

"Boy, things sure do look different
When my head is near the ground.
I will spend the day like this
And have a look around."

So Tracy got right out of bed
As happy as could be,
Glad to have a brand-new day
To see what she could see.

Tracy knew at breakfast time
Her mom might throw a fit;
Her head was down, her bottom up.
"Now that's no way to sit!"

Have you ever eaten pancakes
When your bottom is on top?
It's an upside-down phenomenon
To never spill a drop (of syrup, that is).

Now, being an upside-downer
Can hurt your hands and feet,
So on the jungle gym she climbed
And looked out at the street.

There were people driving cars around
With tires in the air.
They all looked kind of funny,
But they didn't seem to care.

Flip and see what Tracy saw!

The birds were flying belly up
With floating clouds below,
And trees were standing on their leaves
Blowing to and fro.

Flip and see what Tracy saw!

Then Tracy saw a brand-new word
Upon a traffic sign...
"D-O-T-S... D-O-T-S,"
She wondered with all her mind.

Flip and see what Tracy saw!

And for a moment . . . just a bit,
She turned herself around.
"Oh, that spells 'stop', not 'dots'," she said.
Then it was back to upside down.

"I'm feeling kind of dizzy.
I wonder why that's so?
Is this what upside-downers feel?
I certainly don't know."

So off the jungle gym she dropped
And landed on the ground.
Ready to check things out again
And have a look around.

"I cannot ride my bike like this,
Or jump rope," she thought.
I cannot play my hopscotch game;
I cannot do a lot."

"There's really not much I can do
On this upside-downer day.
No wonder God created us
In a right-side-upper way!"

"I like living right side up,
The way it's meant to be.
It's my face God sees and not my feet
When he's looking down at me!"

So the upside-down adventure
Had finally come to rest,
And Tracy realized that day
That God's way is the best!